For Pants-tastic Gabriel ~ CF

For Dave ~ BC

ALADDIN

An imprint of Simon & Schuster Children's Publishing Division

1230 Avenue of the Americas, New York, NY 10020

Text copyright © 2008 by Claire Freedman

Illustrations copyright © 2008 by Ben Cort

Originally published in Great Britain in 2008 by Simon & Schuster UK Ltd.

First U.S. Edition, 2010

Manufactured in the United States of America

First Aladdin hardcover edition January 2010.

8 10 9

Library of Congress Control Number 2009002095

ISBN: 978-1-4169-8938-7

Dinosaurs Love Underpants

ILLUSTRATED BY
Ben Cort

CLAIRE FREEDMAN

aladdin
NEW YORK   LONDON   TORONTO   SYDNEY

Dinosaurs were all wiped out,
A long way back in history.
No one knows quite how or why,
Now this book solves the mystery...

It all began when cavemen
Felt embarrassed in the nude.
So someone dreamed up underpants
To stop them from looking crude.

The dinosaurs roamed everywhere,
All teeth and huge long necks,
But scariest and meanest
Was Tyrannosaurus rex!

When T. rex saw Man's undies,
He roared with deafening rants,
"I don't want to eat you up,
I want your underpants!"

T. rex stole a furry pair,

But his briefs quickly ripped.

He couldn't get them past his feet.

Oh! Whoops! Watch out! He tripped!

Triceratops was happy,
Wearing undies on every horn,
Till Styracosaurus snatched them
And they ended up all torn.

The pants from Woolly Mammoth coats
Made Stegosaurus itchy.
Diplodocus was really mad.
His briefs were way
    too pinchy!

"We're running low on underpants!"
The cavemen quaked in shock.
"These dinos are undies crazy.
They've completely run amok!"

Soon undies were flying everywhere,
All torn by tooth and claw.
The dinosaurs were fighting
In a great briefs tug-of-war.

The Mighty Underpants War raged all night,
THUMP, POW, BASH, THWACK, CLOUT!
The fighting got so crazy,
All the dinos were wiped out!

The next day, out the cavemen crept,
And cheered at what they saw.
"Hooray! Our biggest enemy
Is now at last no more!"

So when you put your undies on,
Always treat them with great care.
Don't forget briefs saved Mankind.
They're not just underwear!